Contenders of the Last Will

Book One

Valeria Sweet

ISBN: 9798985473018

Cover art by: Maria Oglesby
Photo in About the Author by: Michael Roud
Printed in the United States of America

Contents

Title Page

Copyright

Introduction

Chapter One   1

Chapter One   3

Chapter Two   17

Chapter Two   19

Chapter Three   29

Chapter Three   31

Chapter Four   39

Chapter Four   41

Chapter Five   51

Chapter Five   53

Chapter Six   63

Chapter Six   65

About The Author   75

Introduction

Dear Reader,

It's such an honor to be read by you! Thank you for picking up this book! If you're unfamiliar with the journey Contenders took to get here, I'd love to tell you the story of how this project came to be, so you understand the format it's written in.

Originally, Contenders was a ten-episodes series written for television that was pitched around Hollywood 2017-2018. We filmed an amazing Promo for it, which served as an extended first-look trailer. Everyone loved it, alas it's an Original work. You see, series like Contenders have usually been a book series or comics first, i.e. Vampire Diaries, Pretty Little Liars, Riverdale, etc.

At that time, I'd never written a book and didn't know how to reverse-engineer a script into published fiction. Since then, I've published three self-help books, filmed a mini-series, a pilot, and a feature film that I wrote, directed, acted in, and produced. I got busy, but never forgot about Contenders.

Fast forward to now, Contenders reclaims its space and becomes a book series, starting with Book One. Based on the Pilot script, structurally it might appear different from a regular fiction book that wasn't a script first. It won't bore you with flowery descriptions, as it will be dialog-focused. Imagine watching a one-hour drama on CW, Freeform, or Netflix in book form.

Based on my high school experience, Contenders has a special place in my heart. I grew up watching Buffy the Vampire Slayer, whose friendships and honesty were comforting to watch. You weren't just watching a show, you were really there with them. I hope to relay that feeling in my work as well. I hope you enjoy Contenders as much as I did creating it, and that it gets made soon for you to watch on TV!

– Valeria Sweet

Chapter One

VALERIA SWEET

Chapter One

Anabelle Ascher, a beautiful widow in her forties, dressed in an all-black Victorian dress, rushes around gathering her things all over the Ascher estate, her Victorian mansion. She throws a suitcase toward the door. Another suitcase goes flying. She stops by the desk and takes out two documents. With one document in hand, she hurries into the beautiful Gallery Room.

William, a local newspaper boy of fifteen years of age, runs into the house, "Mrs. Ascher, we have to go! They're here!"

Anabelle rushes out of the Gallery.

"I don't quite have everything packed, but I know, I know..."

He takes her suitcases and they rush out of the house into the woods. Out of nowhere – SHOTS FIRE AT THEM.

Willam screams, "Madam!"

They jolt toward the bushes to hide from the shots. Anabelle turns to William.

"I knew this was going to happen! You have to go!"

"I promised I'd stay with you!"

"We will see each other very soon."

She reaches urgently into her purse and hands him a document – it's her will.

"This is for the future generations – to preserve and remember the history of it all... we can't take it to our graves." She pauses. "You are the heir. Take this to Mr. Garfield - our attorney - he knows. Then come straight to our place in the woods."

He takes the will.

"I will do as you say."

"I want you to remember that everything I did was to protect you from the Trustees. Now we have to make sure they can never have what lawfully belongs to us. Some day our family will be able to come back home."

He hugs her tight.

More shots fire at them.

Anabelle urges William, "Go!"

"I love you!"

"I love you, too, William."

He sprints towards the back road. She takes her suitcases and runs into the woods, careful not to draw attention to herself.

SIBYLLINE HILLS, CA - PRESENT DAY

The sunny neighborhood of an old money small suburban town of Sibylline Hills resembles mansions of Hancock Park, with houses one bigger than another. Valentina Peterson's, however, is a modest home.

Valentina, sweet-faced, seventeen, and innocent, yet indie rock with a bit of spunk and a lot of curiosity, goes through her closet and picks out a Nirvana T-shirt.

Her room, eclectic with a vintage vibe, has a vanity table, a map, lots of books, and a cork bulletin board with Ascher Estate on it.

Valentina's computer has her blog pulled up - "ASK V."

She sits down and types:

"Dear Anonymous, thank you for your question. Would I recommend shutting yourself off from the rest of the world in hopes of never being heartbroken? Absolutely not. You never know who will come along and when. You get to live and learn, so it's worth it. We can never keep anybody against their will, but it's rewarding to love and we shouldn't deny anyone a chance to know us. I hope this helps. Take care, Ask V."

She clicks "Post," then grabs her bag and heads for the door.

Outside, Valentina sees Max, her eighteen-year-old brooding next-door neighbor. He puts something in his mailbox, then sees Valentina and waves. She hesitates but waves back.

Sammy, a sixteen-year-old with a girl-next-door feel, armed with sarcasm and anxiety, picks Valentina up in her old Volkswagen Beetle. Sammy notices her shirt.

"Paying homage to the late Kurt, I see."

"Something like that."

Sammy looks in Max's direction.

"He's so in love with you."

"Who Max? No..."

"You're in denial. Just look at him. I bet he waited outside for you to come out."

Changing the subject, Valentina picks up Sammy's notebook.

"Did you write another chapter?"

"Yeah, stayed up so late, I think I got carpal tunnel."

"You didn't."

Sammy smirks.

"No, I didn't. My mom made me go to bed before that could happen."

"I'm proud of you for writing every waking hour. For what it's worth, I think you'll become a famous author."

"Aww, thanks, V. Maybe our "Oliver With a Twist" book will become a New York Times Best Seller."

They chuckle.

Sammy continues, "Speaking of that, have you heard from Oliver?"

"Nope."

"Last time I saw his updates, he was in New York or something."

"Oh yeah? Good for him. I hope he finds what he's looking for."

Valentina and Sammy arrive at the school and split going to their lockers.

Valentina gets some books out. As she turns, she sees Dylan, a confident and quiet handsome reformed bad boy, eighteen years of age. He wears a Nirvana T-shirt – just like hers. He passes by and as if time slowed down, their eyes meet for a prolonged moment. Valentina doesn't dare to breathe.

Sammy returns to Valentina.

"I saw that! Who was that?"

"You don't know him?"

"Should I?"

"No, I mean... I've seen him a couple of times around the neighborhood, but I didn't know he went here."

"You probably just never noticed him. You know, Oliver and all."

"No... I don't think that's it..."

Valentina follows Sammy into the school library and Sammy gets out the school's yearbook. They skim the pages – nothing. Valentina stares at the yearbooks from previous years, then takes one out. She guides her index finger through photos until she stops.

"Got him. Dylan Rushmore."

Sammy points out a photo of a girl on the same page.

"Oh, and look, your "bestie" Briana was in the same grade."

Valentina and Sammy come out of the library into the school hallway and meet up with their friend Quentin, a protective, yet self-conscious, hipster, also eighteen.

Valentina turns to him.

"Q, do you know Dylan Rushmore?"

He looks around.

"Not really. Why?"

"I don't remember him from last year but we saw him this morning and..."

"Actually, sorry, I forgot, I have to get to class early."

He turns to Sammy.

"Are you coming?"

Sammy nods but Valentina holds them up.

"Well, can we still go to the Old Town Library after school? I've been wanting to see it for ages."

Quentin starts to leave.

"Yeah, sure. I'll let my mom know we're stopping by."

Sammy walks after him.

"See you after, V!"

As they leave, Briana, a gossip queen at seventeen years old, with a side of a saboteur, walks up to Valentina. Briana wears PJs yet looks all dolled up, "I thought you were doing Spirit Week with me."

"Eh... I didn't feel like just rolling out of bed this morning."

"Well, obviously you don't just roll out of bed."

"But then it doesn't make sense to be wearing sleeping clothes and doing hair and makeup."

"So? Have some school spirit."

"I'll do Decade Day."

"You better. And it better not be the 20's, because that's what I'm doing."

"Don't... worry."

"Oh, here."

Briana gets a perfume bottle out of her purse and sprays Valentina with it. Valentina ducks away.

"Hey!"

The girls giggle. Briana hands Valentina the perfume bottle.

"I bought two so we could match. Twins!"

"Wow, thanks, B!"

Valentina puts the perfume in her bag.

"By the way, do you know Dylan Rushmore?"

Briana stares, quick on her answer:

"Do you like him or something?"

"No, I don't even know him."

Briana winks playfully.

"Well... you better get with him before I do."

"Briana..."

Briana smiles.

"Take a joke! You're so serious. I know you're not over Oliver."

Briana turns to leave. Her perky expression

changes to grim.

Later that morning, Valentina shelves books at the library when Max sneaks up on her.

"Valentina."

She jumps.

"Sorry," he mutters.

"Hey, Max."

"Hey, I was just wondering if you're free tonight?"

She keeps shelving the books.

"Why, what's up?"

"Oh, I just thought we could see a movie or something."

She shifts.

"Oh... Oh, I'm hanging out with Sammy and Quentin."

He slowly starts backing out of the conversation:

"I get it. Friends."

"...I'm sure we can maybe hang out some other time?"

"Yeah! For sure. Let me know."

He smiles and walks off, as Jake, an eighteen-year-old skater kid, passes by.

"Hey V!"

Valentina blurts out, "Jake, do you by any chance know Dylan Rushmore?"

"Uh, yeah... he's my best friend."

In shock, "Wait, what? Really?"

"Want me to introduce you?

"...Yeah!"

"Come to the courtyard during lunch."

He walks out of the library, leaving Valentina stunned.

At lunch, Valentina comes out to the school courtyard. There are only a few students there. When she sees Dylan and Jake walk out of the school, she zips up her hoodie to hide the Nirvana T-shirt, a little embarrassed. As they walk up to her, Dylan stops, but Jake keeps walking by:

"Valentina, Dylan. Dylan, Valentina. I'm gonna go finish my lunch. Have fun you two!"

Dylan smiles.

"Valentina, that's a pretty name."

"Thanks, it was my grandmother's. You can just call me V, that's what my friends call me."

"V. Got it."

He pauses.

"Hey... you're the one with the Nirvana shirt."

She nods, feeling embarrassed again.

"Yeah, you too..."

"Is Nevermind your favorite album?"

"I like In Utero better... Oh, sorry, I'm really not trying to be pretentious! Nevermind is perfect, it just doesn't inspire me quite the same."

"It's okay! That's my favorite album, too."

"Really? Don't meet that many In Utero lovers around here."

He chuckles.

"Yeah, I totally get you there."

11

"I didn't know you were friends with Jake."

"Yeah, he's my brother. Some friends are better than family."

She nods.

Dylan continues, "You know, I knew we'd meet someday. I've been seeing you around."

Valentina turns her head slightly to the left and smiles in wonder. The bell rings.

Dylan walks Valentina to class through the school hallway. Valentina turns to him:

"So what do you do besides school?"

"I work. A lot. My mom thought it'd be a great way to keep me out of trouble. In a way she's right. What about you?"

"I have a blog. It's sort of an advice column actually. People ask for advice on whatever they're going through, relationship or personal stuff."

"I guess people trust you easily. You're like a... confidant for them?"

"I guess so. It's also anonymous, so I think that makes it easier for people to open up."

Sammy and Quentin come out of the classroom. They see Valentina and Dylan walking toward them. Quentin pulls Sammy away and outside into the courtyard. Sammy stops Quentin:

"What was that? I wanted to meet him."

"Then you're not going to like what I'm about to tell you."

He takes a solemn pause.

"I know you and V only transferred to this

district last year, but I've known Dylan since elementary school. He has quite a reputation and has been gone for a year. No idea where. But if I had to bet, his family had him in a boarding school or the psych ward."

"Harsh! What happened?"

"I saw him lose it on someone in our school. Like blood everywhere. Poor kid."

"No way... Shouldn't you be telling V all of this?"

"I know how she is, she gives everyone the benefit of the doubt. You have to help me get this message across."

As Dylan leaves Valentina by her locker, Briana watches them and follows Dylan out into the parking lot. She catches up to him.

"Didn't know you were back in school. Missed me?"

He sees her and keeps walking.

"What do you want?"

"That's not a way to greet a lady."

"Do we have to do this?"

"Do what?"

"Interact."

"Ouch! Okay. I'll get straight to the point then. Leave her alone."

He stops in his tracks.

Briana continues, "She's not like you and me. She's different. She's a little goody-two-shoes."

"What is it that you think I'm after?"

She stares at him.

"I told you I wasn't interested in getting back together and I'm still not."

"If I can't change your mind, I guess I'll have to change hers."

"Now that would be tragic if you could influence someone so genuine. Maybe you should learn from her."

"Oh, yeah? And what should I learn? How to have a rebound relationship?"

"What does that have to do with anything?"

"I guess that's for you to find out."

She walks off leaving him wondering what she was talking about.

Chapter Two

Chapter Two

NEW YORK CITY, NEW YORK - PRESENT DAY

The same day, in a dim old-timey office den with decorative mahogany furniture, someone goes quickly through leather-bound journals inside a heavy-duty desk. It's Violet, mysterious and enigmatic, in her early twenties and in all black, like a stealthy, but stylish, ninja. There's a knock on the door. She surely didn't expect anyone. She goes to the door and slowly cracks the door open. A young man, of about nineteen years of age, looks at her, confused. He seems charming but detached, a bit of a lone-wolf type.

"Mrs... Schwartz?"

"...Sure. How may I help you?" Violet replies.

"I heard you specialize in different... societies?"

Violet looks him up and down, assessing the situation.

"Does it have anything to do with the Old

Town Library?"

"How...?"

"Please, come in."

She lets him in and moves back toward the desk.

"Scotch or gin?"

He looks around. Clearly not 21.

"Scotch would be fine. Thanks."

Violet pushes the journals into the drawer and flips down a framed picture of Mrs. Schwartz on the desk with one hand, simultaneously picking up a bottle with another. She hands him a glass and offers a seat across the desk that she leans on. She toasts.

"To your dad, may he rest in peace."

He looks down.

"My condolences. I figured you wouldn't be here if your dad was still a Trustee."

Alarmed by the word, he looks back up at Violet.

***

After school, at the Old Town Library, Valentina walks around the European Art wing of the Ascher Estate. It resembles the Huntington Library. This wing is well-lit and welcoming, despite the relatively unkempt building. She walks into the Gallery Room where one painting has people gathered around. The curator, Mrs. Eve Castellane, or Mrs. C, a poised and self-assured woman in her forties, talks to the crowd about an unassuming landscape painting with a scenery of a forest:

"This painting was finished in 1717. For a long time, we thought it was just one coat of paint, but in 1943 an X-ray showed there was a painting prior to the one we see now. Then, in the year 2000, we also discovered there was a third painting on this canvas..."

Valentina finds Sammy and Quentin.

"I just love old mansions. I wonder what kind of secrets this one holds."

Sammy replies, "I think you've done too many escape rooms. No one's lived here since, like, the early 1900s. I'm sure they moved every rock and tourists looked under it too."

Mrs. C moves on. Valentina moves closer to the painting:

"Really wouldn't have guessed there were paintings on top of paintings..."

"That was probably the point...," Quentin smirks.

Valentina examines the intricate framework of the painting. She notices a little tab on its side that is not seen from looking at the front of the frame. She looks around, then feels a cut-out for a button by the bottom of the frame. She presses the button. A small drawer opens up and rolled-up parchment falls out.

Valentina whispers, "Guys..."

She opens up the parchment. Sammy and Quentin surround her. Quentin seems to recognize it.

"It looks like Mrs. Ascher's Will…"

Quentin turns to get Mrs. C's attention:

"Hey, Mom…"

Sammy takes a quick photo of the note. Mrs. C swiftly walks toward them and sees the Will.

"Where did you find that?"

Quentin starts, "Valentina just pressed on the frame…"

Mrs. C, quick on her feet, snatches the will and urges them to leave:

"Go home. All of you. NOW!"

Valentina, Sammy, and Quentin hurry toward the Old Town Library parking lot.

Sammy asks, "How did you even think to look at the frame?"

"I guess there was so much attention on the painting, that I was drawn to the frame instead," Valentina replies.

They get to Sammy's car and look at the photo of the will. Sammy reads:

"Last Will and Testament: I declare this to be my Last Will. Mr. Arthur Garfield has the detailed copy in which I leave everything to my Heir, William Draft, upon reaching the age of eighteen. He will know what to do with the inheritance. If he, for any reason, is unable to collect it, everything shall go to the Contender who collects all of my most important personal possessions found at the Estate and on the property. Signed: Anabelle Ascher

Oct. 21st 1910. Witnesses: Samuel Graystone and Margarette Scott."

Valentina looks at Sammy and Quentin:

"Anabelle was the owner of the Old Town Library?"

"Yeah. She was the richest woman at the end of the nineteenth century," Quentin jumps in.

"Who runs it now?"

"The Trustees appointed by Mr. Ascher before his death."

Sammy turns to Quentin:

"Can anyone become a Contender?"

"Only the people who know about the will," he replies.

The girls, big-eyed, stare at Quentin. He looks around and lowers his voice:

"What you just found is not meant to be public. Technically anyone can become an heir as long as they know what they're looking for, but that's the Trustees' insider information. It's a dangerous world and I try to stay away from it as far as possible."

"So are we not supposed to know about this?" Valentina asks.

"Just promise me not to tell anyone about it."

They all silently exchange glances.

***

Back in the old-timey office, the young man looks out the window when Violet walks up. He turns to her:

"The Will states that anyone can become a Contender."

"Yes... But you are one of the Trustees. You already own it," Violet replies.

"But we can't do anything with it as Trustees."

"Right... So you want to have it all for yourself? What if there's an heir already?"

"Then they'll have to contend for it as well. But it's just a myth, right? I mean, how can it be that after all these years someone can still be out there and hasn't stepped up?"

She stares at him like a bird of prey.

Violet finally replies, "I've found that anything is possible in this world and nothing should be ruled out."

She pauses.

"What was the circumstance of your father's death?"

"A lot of fathers died in the Old Town Library fire."

She looks at him with grief.

"Did they ever find out what caused the fire?"

"They said it was arson. But they never found out who did it."

He watches her.

Violet continues, "And to avenge your father's death you want to contend... You know it's a path that led a lot of the Trustees astray, some of them have even gone mad."

"If my father wasn't a Trustee, he'd still be here

and I wouldn't have to be one. In that respect, I feel like I'm owed something for losing him so soon," he replies.

"Each family has their own skeletons, huh?"

He steps closer to Violet.

"You know, contending was just an idea before I came here, but I think you, too, believe it's possible to find the inheritance."

She watches him.

"You're not wrong. Not right either."

***

Later that evening, Sammy and Valentina get ready for bed in Valentina's bedroom. Brushing their teeth and dressed in matching PJs by the bathroom mirror, Sammy exclaims:

"You and Dylan... Spill!"

Valentina replies with a toothbrush in her mouth, "We're just getting to know each other."

"Uh-huh... You look like you already know each other."

Valentina smiles coyly.

Sammy continues, "I guess I'll have to tell my mom you're dating now so that she lets me go to the mall by myself."

Valentina laughs.

"You just have to tell her to trust you more. You've never proved her otherwise."

"Yeah, it won't happen overnight..."

The girls finish up getting ready and get into

bed. Sammy points at the Ascher Estate photo from the corkboard:

"I never noticed you had a photo of the Old Town Library."

"Oh yeah, I've been drawn to the Old Town Library for years, and then we moved here, and then the Will..."

"What a day to find it, huh?"

"That's the thing. I almost think I was supposed to find it. It's hard to explain, but ever since I was little, whenever I followed my intuition, everything connected like a web, as if everything around me was a sign."

"Does your intuition tell you that Q and Mrs. C are hiding something?"

"For sure. Q asked us not to tell anyone, but he didn't say we couldn't figure it out ourselves... You have to help me find out the truth about what happened to Anabelle and William. If we don't, I'm not sure anyone ever will."

Sammy nods slowly in realization as Valentina kills the lights.

Chapter Three

Chapter Three

It's Decade Day at school. Dylan, in a leather jacket with hair slicked back, sits on the picnic table in the courtyard. He looks up and sees Valentina walking toward him. She's in an 80's punk outfit of a short black pleated skirt, GBH T-Shirt, fishnets with holes, black boots, and kohl-rimmed eye makeup.

"Badass! You're you, just a more exaggerated version of yourself?"

"Thanks! And you... not quite sure. 90's? 60's?" Dylan chuckles.

"Yeah, I don't even know."

He pauses, smiling.

"Listen, I have a surprise for you."

"Oh... I'm not big on surprises..."

Without further ado, he takes her hand in his and walks her through the courtyard, as if they're an "it" couple, or at least the punk King and Queen of the school. She looks up at him in awe, feeling on cloud nine about this gesture. Is it the next step in the relationship, which is moving faster than she ever expected? Everyone watches Valentina and Dylan walk by, including Max and Briana, who's dressed in her 20's outfit.

In the parking lot, Dylan helps Valentina onto the bed of his pickup truck, making sure she's comfortable. Then, he gets out his guitar and plays the first few chords of "Heart-Shaped Box" by Nirvana. She interrupts him:

"How did you know that's my favorite song?"

"Just a hunch. Or an instinctive feeling of sorts."

"I know that feeling."

He smiles and continues:

"Why didn't we meet before?"

"Oh, I just moved here last year from Virginia," Valentina replies.

"Did you throw darts at the map?"

"I did!"

They laugh.

"Were you aiming for LA and missed?"

"No, I was throwing at the whole United States and it landed here."

"Impressive."

She smiles; then inquires bashfully:

"Did you go here last year? I noticed your picture wasn't in last year's yearbook."

"Curious, aren't we?"

Valentina bites her lip:

"You did ask first…"

He nods.

"The last couple of years were hard for me, so last year I just got home-schooled. Everything is different now though," Dylan replies.

"In a good way?"

"I would like to think so."

He puts his arm around her and she melts into him. They sit there for a long while.

After school, Valentina sits on a bench in front of the school, waiting to get picked up. Briana walks up to her, talking fast:

"I know this is going to sound like it's coming out of nowhere, but I can tell you're falling for him, so just between us, I don't think he's the kind of guy you want."

"What makes you say that?"

"I've seen how head over heels you were for Oliver and I want to save you some heartache. He's worse than Oliver. Dylan is dangerous."

Briana's ride arrives and she starts toward the car. Valentina gets up from the bench and follows Briana:

"Why is he dangerous?"

Briana gets in the car:

"He might not look like it, but he's a psychopath, trust me."

"That's a serious accusation."

Briana stares at Valentina:

"Did he tell you that we dated?"

"...What?"

"I didn't think so."

Briana puts the window up and the car drives off, leaving Valentina perplexed.

Later that afternoon, Valentina, Sammy, and Quentin work on their art projects on the kitchen counters of Quentin's house. They've all been quiet for a while.

Valentina finally speaks, "B was so weird to me today. She said that Dylan is a psychopath."

"Did she say it takes one to know one?" Quentin asks. "Why are you still friends with that Briana-witch?"

"Because when I didn't know anyone here, she was nice to me."

"Ugh, you saying she's nice makes my skin crawl. Well, ask Dylan, I'm sure he can explain."

Sammy interjects, "Q, just tell her."

"Tell me what?"

Quentin hesitates.

Valentina asks Quentin again, "Tell me what, Q?"

Quentin throws a look at Sammy.

"Ahh... Well... He's always been kind of a... jerk? And when his dad died, he sort of went crazy, so his family took him out of school?"

"His dad died?" Valentina asks quietly. "How did his dad die?"

"Both of our dads died in a fire at the Old

Town Library right before you moved here. The fire took out the whole wing of the place, hence the renovation there."

"Oh my God, Q… I had no idea that's how your dad died as well."

"Yeah… It's okay. I've dealt with it better than some of the others. Anyway… The last time I saw Dylan before this year… I didn't want to show you, but I think you should know what happened."

Quentin gets out his computer and pulls up a video taken with a cell phone. In it:

Dylan holds a student, who has his back to us, by his collar. The frame of the video shakes as the onlooker hides. Dylan screams at the student, "Is that what they told you to do or did you come up with it on your own?!" Dylan punches the guy in the face, hard. The guy falls, and Dylan stomps on him over and over again. Voices shout, "Dylan, stop!" The camera quickly points down, gets closer, and shuts off.

Valentina and Sammy look at the video in shock.

"…That was, like, post-traumatic stress, right?" Valentina asks.

Quentin's jaw drops:

"Are you kidding me?! He put someone in the hospital!"

Quentin turns to Sammy.

"See! What did I tell you?"

Concurrently, Mrs. C arrives at the house. She's

in a heated argument on the phone:

"I told you already, there wasn't anything. They just found an old piece of paper. It's a commotion over nothing."

She sees the three teens staring at her from the kitchen.

She continues into the phone, "That's all. Goodbye." She ends the call and walks into the kitchen.

"How are my favorite teenagers?"

"Hi, Mrs. C! Good!" Valentina and Sammy exclaim in unison.

"Another art project?"

The teens nod. Mrs. C looks around.

"Quentin, you didn't offer them anything to drink? Girls, would you like some water or sweet tea?"

"We're okay, Mrs. C..." Valentina replies. "We were, however, wondering about that whole thing at the Old Town Library?"

Quentin and Mrs. C exchange looks. Mrs. C turns to Valentina, dumbfounded:

"What are you talking about?"

"The will that we found?"

"Oh... I took care of it. It's not anything worth discussing."

"Sure it is... we found it..."

Sammy pulls Valentina on the sleeve.

"When are you ladies heading out?" Mrs. C asks.

Sammy quickly replies, "Now, actually."

Valentina and Sammy hurriedly grab their projects and head out the door.

Mrs. C turns to Quentin, "Quentin, what is the matter with you bringing your friends to the Old Town Library in the first place?"

He shrugs.

"I didn't know they weren't allowed in there…"

"The curious ones aren't."

She throws him a look of disbelief.

"You said you didn't want to be a part of it, so stay out of it and make sure they don't find out anything else. Please. For your sake and mine."

"Mom, I'm sorry. I had no idea they were going to ask…"

"I've kept the finding of the Will off the radar, but if the Trustees find out your friends know, there will be consequences, for everyone."

In the driveway, Valentina and Sammy hurry to Sammy's car.

"What's with Mrs. C?" Sammy asks.

"Whatever it is, doesn't sound like she wants us going around saying anything about the Will. Or that we have proof of it."

The girls get in the car and speed away.

Chapter Four

Chapter Four

The same evening, the young man and Violet sit close together on the couch, digging through the old books in the same old-timey office. Violet closes the book she's on but continues watching him flip through the books fast, half-heartedly devouring the knowledge in them.

"What are you looking for, anyway?" Violet asks.

"Anything about the heirs and how to find them."

"I doubt you'll find that written in any books."

"What do you suggest I try?"

"I suggest you don't."

She half-smiles.

"Why?"

"Just a hunch that it won't lead anywhere."

He stops going through the books and looks at her. Then, he brushes her hair back.

"You're a mystery, you know that?"

Violet smiles again.

"And you're a stalker. Why do you keep coming back here?"

"What can I say? I'm just so fascinated with you. How do you know so much about everything?"

"I'm an avid reader."

"Interesting. So what's your stake in all of this?"

"Just want to see who the next heir's going to be. Want the truth to prevail. Just like you, but different."

He's fixated on her now.

"Is it true that your great-grandfather was Mr. Garfield, Anabelle Ascher's attorney? And that your family have since protected the Will and acted in Anabelle's defense when impostor heirs showed up?"

She looks at him not knowing where he's going with this.

"Oh... you mean the Schwartzes... I guess there's no point in denying it if you know."

He locks eyes with her for a long moment. She breaks his concentration by getting up.

"Excuse me."

He watches her leave the room when he hears a faint ringtone coming from her side of the couch. He looks for the cell phone buried in the pillows. The caller – "Mrs. C." He hesitates, then picks up the call.

"Sorry, I've been so busy, I should've called you earlier. My son and his ever-curious friend Valentina found a copy of Anabelle's Last Will and it looks like there are some new details we haven't seen before. ... Violet?"

The young man hangs up the phone, blocks the number, and deletes the call. He hurriedly picks up his jacket and heads for the door.

***

The same night, Valentina and Dylan get coffee at a local coffee shop. Dylan leaves a tip in the jar for the cashier, a plump woman in her fifties. She smiles and addresses Valentina.

"He's a keeper."

Embarrassed, Valentina replies, "Thanks..."

Then, she and Dylan grab the coffee mugs and sit down in a small booth. He watches her put a lot of creamers in her drink.

"Would you like some coffee with your creamer?"

"I know, it's a lot," Valentina replies.

He watches her for a moment. She avoids eye contact.

"Dylan, if you don't want to talk about it, it's okay, but I heard about your dad and I'm sorry you had to go through that."

He gets defensive, "What did you hear?"

"Just that he died in a fire..."

He looks down, she gives him space for a moment.

"Were you really close to him?"

43

"Not as much as I wish I was," Dylan sighs. "He was an example of integrity, you know. I wish I valued it more when he was alive. Listen, I want you to know where I'm coming from. I think it affected me so much because I was supposed to pick him up from a meeting, but that evening I was late, as I used to be a lot at that time in my life…"

Dylan goes down memory lane:

"It was night. I pulled up in my truck toward the road in front of the Old Town Library. The wing of the Old Town Library was burning in flames. I got out of the truck and ran to the burning building. I tried getting through the men standing outside. One of them landed his hand heavily on my shoulder. "Sorry about your father, he was a good man. You will continue his work - you are a part of us now," he told me. And that was that."

Valentina listens to Dylan intently.

"Did he mean… a part of the Trustees?"

"How do you know?" Dylan asks defensively again.

"Quentin mentioned them… So you became one of the Trustees?"

"All of the sons did."

Valentina gasps:

"… so Quentin?…"

"Yeah. There were a few from our school. But I'm not a part of it anymore. I'd stay away from all of this if I were you."

Dylan looks at the clock:

"I really need to get you home so I can get in

good with your parents, huh?"

Outside of her house, Valentina gets out of Dylan's car and shivers. He gets out a jacket – the marine corps fatigues.

Valentina asks, "Marine Corps?"

"It's from a summer thing I did with my dad." He helps her put the jacket on. The jacket says "RUSHMORE."

"For some reason, I didn't take you for one following the rules."

"You're right, I'm not, but I do like some structure. I come from a military family, and it's a way of staying connected to my dad. You should keep the jacket, you look good in it."

She smiles.

"Thanks. Well, goodnight," Valentina murmurs and hugs Dylan.

"Sleep tight. Don't let those bed bugs bite."

Valentina heads for the house as Dylan pulls out of the driveway. Max watches them from a distance.

Valentina walks into the house, greeted by Sofia, her enthusiastic, cool mom in her late thirties.

"Who was that handsome fellow?"

Valentina smiles big.

"His name is Dylan."

"Does he have a swarm of girls after him?"

"Not that I know of. Although my friends don't

seem too excited about him."

"Well, you know what they say, there is no smoke without fire."

"Um, not a great analogy, Mom. His dad died in a fire..."

"Oh, I'm very sorry to hear that! Is Dylan okay?"

Valentina takes off Dylan's jacket.

"Yeah. Now he is."

"What about you? How is school? I don't get to see you as much anymore. You're all growing up."

Sofia hugs Valentina.

"It's been picking up. I think this year will be better than last."

"If you ever need anything, you know you can come to me. I know it can be hard navigating the world at your age. I remember what it was like falling in love with your father..."

"Mom..."

Valentina's cell phone rings. She picks it up, it's Max:

"Hey, can you come outside for a minute? I just want to talk to you about something."

Valentina sighs.

Max waits for Valentina outside and looks very anxious. She finally comes out of the house:

"What's up?"

Max starts, "You're one of my better friends and I don't want anything bad to ever happen to you..."

"Thank you... Why would anything bad happen to me?" Valentina asks.

Max gets flustered.

"It... it might if you keep hanging around Dylan."

"Max, this is vague... if you'd like to unload some kind of baggage on me..."

"Baggage?! How's this for baggage?! He's terrorized and belittled me since fourth grade! Tortured me every day and made fun of me. Told me no girl'd ever look at me. Then last year when my dad died..."

"Your dad died, too? Max, I'm so sorry to hear about this... But Dylan's dad..."

"So what? It makes it okay just because we share a point of intersection?"

Sofia hears them from the house and comes outside:

"Hi... Max. What's going on?"

"Sorry. It's nothing, I was just leaving," Max replies.

He starts walking toward his house.

Valentina shouts to Max, "See you tomorrow!"

"What was that about?" Sophia asks.

"Just like I said, my friends are not too thrilled about Dylan."

Later that night, in bed, Valentina scrolls through photos on her phone and stops on the photo of the Will that Sammy sent her. She opens her computer, then types in the Google search bar

– "Anabelle Ascher." Photos of the beautiful widow dressed in all black come up. She seems to be looking right at Valentina.

Valentina looks through the articles about Anabelle. "Richest woman of her time." "Mrs. Anabelle Ascher never returned home, still deemed alive." "Phantom of the Old Town Library?"

Valentina searches again – "Old Town Library Fire." Multiple news sources come up. She skims the pages. "Arson." "Who could do something like that?" "No suspects." She zooms in on one of the photos from the incident and sees Dylan at the scene. Examining it further, she sees Max there as well.

"Max is also a son of the Trustees?! What is this, six degrees of separation??" Valentina asks out loud.

Valentina types in, "Ascher, Old Town Library, Trustees." A small number of results come up. There's an old photo of the original Trustees with Mr. Ascher. "Mr. Ascher appointed five Trustees to look after the property in case of his death." "Old Town Library remains in limbo. Heir rumored to exist." Valentina types in, "William Draft." No results.

She gives up and tries to sleep, but keeps tossing and turning all night, dreaming the strangest dream. In a dark underground cave, Dylan, Max, and Quentin stand in a right triangle formation around Valentina. A fourth figure in a dark hooded robe appears from the other side. The figure concludes with a perfect square around

Valentina. They begin to chant a part of the Will, "...Everything shall go to the Contender who collects all of my most important personal possessions..."

Valentina jolts awake, pulls up the photo of the Will on her phone, zooms in, and notices a sequence of numbers. She types them into Google Maps – it's a location in a foreign country. She puts a negative sign in front of the Longitude, 34, -118, and types it into Maps again – a forest by the Old Town Library comes up. Her eyes grow big.

Chapter Five

Chapter Five

The next day in the school courtyard, Valentina sees Quentin and Sammy walking out of a building. Valentina approaches Quentin:

"Did you find out anything else about why your mom didn't want us talking about the will?"

"It's fine, V. My mom gets weird sometimes."

"So has she taken matters into her own hands?"

"Are you accusing my mom of stealing property?"

"No! But I just don't understand why she wants us to keep quiet..."

"I asked you to not talk about it. I've already said too much as is. If you keep digging deeper, there will be consequences for all of us. Just stop trying to figure it out like it's our business. It's not!"

Quentin walks off. Concerned Sammy follows,

leaving Valentina alone again. Valentina walks off to her locker wearing Dylan's jacket with his last name mounted on her chest. Students whisper about her and a teacher gives her a condescending look. Briana walks up to Valentina:

"You know, I was trying to explain it to you in easy terms, but I don't think you understand how serious it is. You see everybody staring at you, right? I told you, Dylan is no angel. Now you're tainted, too."

"He's changed."

"Wow! Changed? So you think people can change? What about Oliver, huh? You're going to take him back, too, if he says he's changed? Also, it's against the rules of friendship to date your friend's ex, so choose wisely."

Briana walks off.

Valentina sighs to herself, "Oh, brother."

She walks into the library, where Max waves her over:

"I'm sorry about last night."

"It's fine," Valentina replies.

"I was just…"

He notices the name tag on her jacket. He points to it.

"What is that?"

She looks down and covers it.

"Nothing."

"I'm not stupid. I told you how I felt about him and you disregarded everything…"

"He's a completely different person now…"

"You're defending him! You just met the guy and you're going to choose him over your friends?"

"You should've told me everything before!"

"I buried it inside me! I just couldn't keep my mouth shut anymore! I thought I could trust you and that you'd understand, but I can just see you being drained of everything you are! Once I wanted to kill myself, but Dylan almost did it for me..."

A teacher shushes them. The few students that are in the library stare at them.

Valentina gasps, "Oh, God... It was you, wasn't it? Dylan put you in the hospital?..."

Max just stares at her. Unable to process it, Valentina runs out of the library.

Dylan finds Valentina sitting outside of the school, on the ground, with her back to the wall. Valentina's eyes are puffy.

"I got your text. Are you okay?" he asks and sits beside her.

Her voice trembles:

"Before I met you, I didn't know much about you and when I asked around no one knew anything, or at least pretended. And I thought no news was good news. But now everyone's whispering behind my back and my friends are telling me to pick between them and you. Are the rumors even true?... I can't do this!"

She begins to sob.

"I'm sorry. I know how you feel and I have to live with that person. You can at least get out when you want."

He gets up and walks off. She buries her face in her arms.

At lunch, Valentina waits for Dylan in the courtyard but he doesn't show.
She searches for him, finally finding him in a classroom with his English teacher, Ms. Evans, early thirties. Valentina knocks on the open door:

"Hi, Ms. Evans. Could I borrow Dylan for a minute?"

"Hi Valentina, of course."

Dylan and Valentina walk out of the classroom into the hallway.

"Walk with me?" says Valentina.

"I thought you ended this."

"No! That's not what I meant this morning. I was just so frustrated with everyone. I should've told you sooner that people were talking, I just thought I could handle it myself."

"Was one of them Briana?"

"Yeah."

"Don't listen to her. I don't."

"But you guys dated?"

"Is that what she called it? She comes up with story after story. We went out a couple of times and she became really obsessive, jealous. Just a can of worms. She still is."

"And what about Max?" Valentina asks quietly.

"Ah, I see."

They sit down on a bench.

"I can only imagine what he had to say. Remember when you asked me about the Trustees? That incident had to do with them. They thought I was up to something, so they sent Max to provoke me. They wanted me out and fortunately for them, but unfortunately for me, I had real anger issues at the time, so I took it out on Max. Things happened since then that have changed me and humbled me and I'd like to think I'm on the right path. Whatever the worst thing I did was, I got it back tenfold. I gained a new perspective on life, grew up, and... couldn't relate to the people here anymore... I can tell you don't know what that's like, I hope you never do. All I can say is, I care about you and I hope you're not one of the things I have to lose too."

She puts her hand on his:

"I really don't know what that was like for you. I'm just glad it's over. I wish everyone else knew it too."

"Me, too. Are you free tonight?"

"I have to meet Sammy for a bit and then Q has a party. I wish I could invite you."

"No, that's okay. I understand not everyone is happy I'm back. I'll work hard to earn their trust again."

"They'll have to accept you sooner or later."

They look into each other's eyes for a moment. Valentina interrupts it:

"Well, I have to head out."

"Sure, I'll see you."

"See you. Bye."

Valentina gets up and starts walking away, looking back at Dylan. He motions a phone with his hand to his ear.

"Call me!"

She laughs:

"I will!"

Later that day, Valentina and Sammy arrive at the Old Town Library and take the path through the woods. Valentina uses her phone's GPS to find the coordinates.

"Great," Sammy blurts out. "And now we're leaving school early to go geocaching for an old dead lady. I'm going to be so grounded."

"Do you want someone else to get to it first?" asks Valentina.

Sammy rolls her eyes.

"No, but this is private property."

"Not exactly. Reading between the lines of what Q said, it's as public as it gets. And also, wills are public, so relax."

"Alright. But you have to go to Q's party tonight. You guys are driving me nuts having me in the middle of this."

"I know. I'll go. But listen. Q, Dylan, and Max's dads all died in that Old Town Library fire and then all of them became sons of the Trustees. It's starting to sound like a secret society type of thing."

"V, that's bonkers. Is everyone a Trustee in this town?"

"All of the guys we know it seems."

Valentina stops in the middle of the three trees, like the right triangle from her dream:

"We're here."

They look around. Sammy notices a mark on a tree:

"Someone was interested in etching."

Valentina points to the marks around the trees spiraling downward. They see the final mark that points under one of the trees. Valentina gets small gardening tools out of her backpack.

"Really?" Sammy asks. "Can I just point out that if we don't find anything, I will feel really silly."

"Don't be a diva. Help me."

They dig until they hit something in the ground. It's a big root.

"And... that was a bust," Sammy moans.

Valentina continues digging around the root. Finally, she hits something else. She gets the dirt out with her hands. Directly under the root of the tree is a small golden box. The girls look at each other in awe.

Sammy exclaims, "Is this our first clue?"

"I guess, but what is it?"

They examine the ornate box. It seems to be made out of a solid piece of gold. Valentina cleans it up with a towel. They try to look for a way to open the box, but it doesn't budge.

Sammy suggests, "Maybe it's not supposed to open. Maybe it's a part of something?"

"Or maybe the design on it is the key," guesses Valentina.

"Or maybe it's a puzzle. I can see if I can find something on it at the library."

Valentina sticks the box in her backpack and looks around:

"That would be great. Until we find out more, don't tell Q."

Sammy nods.

***

Simultaneously, at the Old Town Library's basement, Quentin stands by himself waiting around for someone. He checks the clock – 6 pm. Max enters:

"Did you call this meeting?"

"I called it," says the voice behind them.

Quentin and Max turn around to look. Dylan enters. They avoid eye contact.

Dylan continues, "I know both of you don't want to be here. I don't know if I've ever said it, but I'm truly sorry for the hell I've put you both through. But this isn't about me. All of us care about Valentina and don't want to see her get hurt. She's been asking questions about the Trustees and inferred that we're a part of them."

"She found the Will," says Quentin.

"What? How could you let that happen?" Dylan scolds.

"It wasn't my fault."

Dylan shakes his head.

"Two of us have been out of the Trustees for a while. It leaves you, Max, to watch over that they don't find out about her, while Quentin and I will make sure she doesn't search for more."

Quentin nods:

"Sounds like a plan."

Max turns to Quentin:

"No, it doesn't! It sounds like we're told what to do again." He then shifts to Dylan, "You haven't changed. Whatever bond you think we shared isn't there anymore."

"So you're not going to help?" Dylan asks.

"I'll help her. But on my own terms," says Max. He starts to leave but then stops, "And remove me from your call list. I don't need any more spam."

Max leaves. Quentin and Dylan exchange glances.

"You trust him?" asks Quentin.

"No, but we don't have another way in," Dylan replies. "Take care of Valentina tonight."

Dylan takes off.

"Oh, I will," says Quentin with a smirk.

Chapter Six

Chapter Six

That night at Quentin's house, you could spot a party half a mile away. Cars parked on both sides of the road, music blasting.

"Good thing we don't have neighbors," Quentin says laughing to guests rolling in a beer keg.

"Do you think we should wake up V now?" asks Sammy walking up.

"Oh, yeah, I forgot she's still asleep. A little surprising with how loud it is."

"She had quite a day, I don't blame her. She passed out the minute we got here."

"I'll go get her," says Quentin walking into the house.

"Wake up, sleepy head!" yells Quentin over house music.

Valentina wakes up in a dark bedroom with Quentin on top of her, shaking her by the arms.

"What are you doing?" Valentina asks.

"There's a surprise waiting for you in the living room."

"You know I don't like surprises."

"I know, but it's a "some" one."

"Who?"

"Someone you like. A lot."

"You invited Dylan…?"

"Oliver's here!" Quentin exclaims with ta-da arms in the air.

"What?!"

She's awake now.

"Come on. Now you have to surprise him."

Quentin takes her by the arms and pulls her from the bed toward the living room.

Still in an almost dream state, Valentina enters the house party atmosphere. Indie music plays loudly. Teens dance, eat, drink, and socialize. Oliver, nineteen, sits in a chair with his back to her. As Valentina walks over, Sammy leans in and whispers:

"Close his eyes."

Valentina steps toward where Oliver sits and covers Oliver's eyes with her hands.

"Mmm, wonder who that is," Quentin taunts.

"Who is it?" asks Oliver.

Quentin whispers something to Valentina. Valentina rolls her eyes but succumbs to peer pressure. She leans in and slowly licks Oliver's right ear. He shifts in his chair as the crowd around them reacts:

"Oooh!"

He takes her hands off his eyes and turns around, surprised to see Valentina. She half-smiles, unamused, and walks out of the house. Oliver follows Valentina out on the porch.

"Are you mad at me?" he asks.

"No, just need some air."

"I missed you."

"That's good."

"Why are you being this way?"

"Oh, I don't know. Maybe because you haven't said a word to me since you graduated?"

"You know it's not like that."

She crosses her arms and turns away from him.

Oliver continues, "I was going away to figure out what I wanted to do with my life."

"And did you?"

"I think so."

"Okay, so why are you still dragging me along?"

"Look at you. More outspoken and yet still the same caring and beautiful girl. I love that about you."

She's silent. Oliver faces Valentina and puts her hair behind her ear. In the distance, a figure takes photos of them. Valentina breaks free of the moment:

"I'm seeing someone."

She walks back into the house, leaving Oliver perplexed outside. Briana walks up to him from the driveway:

"What are you doing here? Trying to ignite the old flame?"

He ignores her snarky remark.

Briana continues, "So tell me, are you going to break them up? Cause I would totally be okay with that."

"Who is she with?"

"Oh, you know, just your favorite person ever - Dylan."

He shakes his head in disbelief.

"Whatever. I'm not really here for that."

"So you are just dragging her along."

"No, I'm not!"

"Oh, good. Because she's my friend and I don't want to see her go through that again. On the other hand, I feel like Dylan would be better off with me. What do you think?"

"Don't ask me about anything to do with him."

"Oh, right. Family Feud," Briana mocks him.

Inside the house, Valentina pulls aside an inebriated Quentin:

"Please tell me he's not staying the night."

"I'm not carrying the burden of someone drinking and driving," Quentin replies.

"Oh, but underage drinking is okay?"

"You need to lighten up."

"If you want him to sleep over, maybe he should sleep in your bed."

"What is that supposed to mean?"

Quentin walks off. Sammy walks over to Valentina:

"It must be really confusing with Dylan and Oliver. I'm sure you'll figure it out... but hey, we need more material for our Oliver book! So..."

Quentin shouts, "Everyone, pick a bedroom!"

"Oh, great!" Valentina complains.

"Go get 'em, Tiger! Stay classy, I'll live vicariously through you," says Sammy, patting her on the back.

"You're not staying?"

"No... The principal called my mom and told her we left school early. Oh well, I hope it was worth it. I'll just do some research on that box."

"Thank you, S."

Sammy hugs Valentina and heads out.

Valentina walks into the living room and sees Oliver trying to make himself comfortable sleeping in an armchair. He sees her:

"You can take the couch."

"Oliver..." Valentina starts. "You can come lay on the couch, too."

He looks at her surprised.

"Are you sure?"

She nods:

"Yeah."

He comes over to the couch and lies down beside her, facing her.

"I'm really sorry I hurt you," says Oliver.

"I'm sorry I gave you attitude," Valentina

replies.

They look at each other for a long moment.

"Do you still have feelings for me?" he asks.

She bites her lip.

"Can I kiss you?" he continues.

"Oliver... I don't think we should."

She looks away.

Oliver notes, "That's not a no."

"Oliver, that's not a yes!"

"Is it because of Dylan?" he asks.

"That's not fair. I don't ask who's in your bed."

"Whoa, he's in your bed?"

"That's not what I meant! I just can't do that right now... to him."

"Listen, Dylan isn't..."

"Yeah, yeah, I heard all about it. What do you have against him?"

He looks at her:

"You know what? I'm not going to cloud your mind with it. Just know that I'm always here for you no matter what."

"Thanks... Well, good night."

Valentina starts to turn away from him, but Oliver stops her:

"One last thing... I know you found Anabelle's Last Will."

Hearing those words, adrenaline pulses through her spine. She sits up, ready to flee.

He continues, "It's okay. I'm a Contender."

Her heart pounds harder. She comes to and whispers under her breath:

"You're a son of a Trustee..."

"I am. And now that you know that... How would you like to become one of the Contenders of the Last Will?"

As Valentina processes this information, her eyes question his every word.

***

In a dim, modern New York studio apartment, Violet lies in bed with the journals. She hears a knock on the door. Violet goes to answer – it's Mrs. C.

"Thank goodness! I was worried sick! Why aren't you answering my calls? I'm calling you right now and it's sending me to voicemail."

Mrs. C walks in and shows Violet the phone.

"What in the world? ...That Oliver must've gone through my phone. He's going to hear from me," Violet replies.

"Oliver? Why was he with you?"

"He wanted to see Mrs. Schwartz, to ask her about contending. He's sly but he only thinks he's smart. He doesn't know who he's up against."

"Have you heard from Mrs. Schwartz?"

"No. I'm afraid the Trustees have gotten to her first," Violet says solemnly. "By the time I got here, she wasn't anywhere to be found. I broke into her office to find any clues – found these."

Violet points at the journals and continues:

"That's when Oliver confused me with Mrs. Schwartz, which told me he didn't come from the

Trustees' side. Don't worry, I didn't let on that I knew who he was, but I think he's gone rogue, which may or may not play into our hands."

"He has interesting timing. My son's friend Valentina found the Last Will in the Gallery Room," Mrs. C replies.

She hands Violet the Last Will. Violet takes in the information and stares at the scroll in awe.

"Who's Valentina?" Violet asks.

"Just a teenage girl that's too curious for her own good."

"Do I need to pay her a visit?"

"I told my son to keep her at bay."

Mrs. C pauses.

"Violet, come back with me to Sibylline Hills. I did everything in my power and will continue to protect you. Maybe this time we can piece everything together and you can finally have what belongs to your family."

Violet takes her eyes off the Will and looks up at Mrs. C with Mona Lisa's uncatchable smile.

The End of Book One

About The Author

Valeria Sweet

 Valeria is an actress and director in Los Angeles. Little did she know she'd ever become a writer. Yet, a hidden talent emerged in 2014 when she wrote her first short film. Since then, she's written multiple feature-length scripts and series episodes, most of which can be seen on www.ValeriaSweet.com. Her 4th book, Contenders of the Last Will: Book One, rounds off her literary works that range from self-help to fiction.

She also serves her community as a dream life mentor through her inspirational newsletters. To get on the list, sign up via www.ValeriaSweet.com

Books By This Author

The Most Wanted One In The World: How To Be "The One" To Meet "The One"

Through dating, studying, and observing relationship psychology, as well as extensive coaching of others, Valeria Sweet has been led to help you find the right person faster. She inspires and motivates through her Manifestation Monday newsletter on ValeriaSweet.com, where she writes about relationships, productivity, health, and healthy mindsets.

Book Of Soulmates

How can we prepare for the soulmate connections we're meant to have? Book of Soulmates helps illustrate all soulmate possibilities. This self-development, relationship advice book is Valeria's second work from her love coaching series. She draws on a multitude of valuable cultural perspectives and details examples of different soulmate relationships. Throughout the book, she uses script excerpts from her miniseries Red String of Fate to further exemplify Red String of Fate coincidences, karmic relationships, and twin flame connections.

Monthly Manifestation Productivity Planner

Monthly Manifestation Productivity Planner is a yearly planner that helps you stay on track of your dreams and goals through manifestation and specificity exercises! Each month has a dedicated journal prompt to help you focus on what's important in the present, your vision, your why, and goal-setting. Monthly calendar pages have space to write down your most important tasks under each day and track them as important, completed, migrated, or cancelled. As you fill the planner with your goals, watch your dreams come to life - what you focus on expands, what gets scheduled gets done, and what gets measured grows! Lots of room for journaling and note-taking. Check out ValeriaSweet.com for more books, courses, and films made using manifestations in this planner!